OUT OF THE
APPLE ORCHARD

by Yvonne David
illustrated by Lyn Rodden

ARBITER PRESS
Orlando · New York

since 1989

ARBITER PRESS
Orlando • New York

A portion of the proceeds from the sale of this book will benefit Jewish Family Services, A United Way agency helping nondenominational families in need.

Editor: Erin West
Copy Editor: Bonnie Fesmire
Editorial Coordinator: Christine Blackwell
Editorial Consultant: Rachel Heimovics Braun
Art Director: Kim Prindle

Library of Congress Control Number: 2005929135

ISBN-13: 978-0-9621385-4-6
ISBN-10: 0-9621385-4-1

Printed in the United States of America.

10 9 8 7 6 5 4 3 2 1

For my son, Austin, whose inspiration gave birth to this book

For my husband, Malcolm, who supported me in realizing my dream

For my dad, whose dreams added drama to the story

And in memory of my mother, who added poetry to my prose

ACKNOWLEDGMENTS

Thanks to all on the publishing team for their wonderful expertise. Together they have made this a truly memorable experience. Editorial coordinator Christine Blackwell supplied the knowledge and judgment that made publication of the book possible. Editor Erin Styers West gave the book cohesion and fluidity. Editorial consultant Rachel Heimovics Braun helped immeasurably with historical facts, Yiddish words, and a wealth of other details. Copy editor Bonnie Fesmire not only tightened the prose but also ensured accuracy in matters from historical dates to editorial details. Art Director Kim Prindle brought a unifying vision to the book. Creative consultant Joanne Fink, owner of Lakeside Design, added artistic finesse to the finished product. Eternal thanks go to my sister, international fine artist Lyn Rodden, for her countless hours of hard work. Her illustrations enhanced the setting and brought the characters to life.

Many thanks also go to my great-aunt Rose Davis for her stories of our family heritage from the Old Country, which added authenticity and richness to the characters, and to my cousins Gillian Reichman and Gillian Davis for their help with family recipes as well as familial background. Thanks to cousin Aaron Scholnik for his keen knowledge and understanding.

For their feedback, support, and advice, I am grateful to Marty, Jan, and Maureen Cummins; Barbara Friedman; Helen Goggin; Jack Levitt; Terry Strummer; Christine Warren; Becky Welch; Linda Twardowsky; Gordon Fink; and Arthur Meltz.

In New York City, appreciation goes to Deena Schwimmer of the American Jewish Historical Society for her help with my research, and also to Yishaya Metal and Hershl Glasser of YIVO Institute for Jewish Research for clarification of Yiddish words.

I am thankful to local librarians Debbie Frank, Joan Mansson, and Steven Jefferies of Maitland Public Library for their valuable assistance with my research and in obtaining much-needed books.

The Catskills connection includes Dr. Phil Brown, president and co-founder of the Catskills Institute and Professor of Sociology at Brown University; John Conway, author and historian for Sullivan County; Helen Kutsher of Kutshers Country Club as well as Joan Schauer and Bob Stein; librarian Alan Barish; author Clarence Steinberg; Charlie Blume, expert on antique apples; and last but not least, Ken and Barbara Schmitt of Mountaindale, New York. A thousand thanks go to them all.

From Congregation of Reform Judaism, great thanks go to Elana Walzer for asking me to write a Jewish High Holidays book at the outset. Most grateful appreciation goes to Rabbi Steven Engel for his spiritual insight and advice.

CONTENTS

The First Bite

Night disappeared as light hovered over the horizon. Soon splinters of sunlight pierced the lace curtains of the Bieman home. It was not the light that awakened young Adam, but rather the hollow aching in his stomach. In his hunger, he hardly noticed the beauty of the reddish-pink glow of sunrise pouring onto the village of Mountaindale, nestled in the blue shadows of the Catskill Mountains.

A quiet stillness enveloped the household, broken only by the intermittent coughing of Adam's father. Getting up and dressed, Adam sighed as he took a broom and began sweeping the wooden plank floor as quietly as possible. Both his younger sister, Sarah, and his grandmother slept unbothered. His mother was already busy making bread. Somehow, the lump of dough she was kneading seemed smaller today.

A whooshing sound outside made Adam spin towards the window. He watched the leaves from the trees plop to the ground like raindrops. Birches, maples, oaks, and hemlocks, exploding in autumnal colors, lined the landscape. He knew that all too soon the trees would be stripped bare, with the rich foliage turning brown on the forest floor. The cold winter lay around the corner. It would be a harsh season to survive in upstate New York.

All of a sudden, Papa coughed so hard that the iron headboard shook. His gasps for breath seemed amplified inside the little frame house. Even the wild oxeye daisies quivered in the vase on his wooden bedside table.

"*Oy gvald!*" said Mama, running to bring him a glass of water. "You sound so bad that I wouldn't wish your cough even on those menacing Russian Cossacks."

Adam dropped the broom and rushed to Papa's side. He looked down at his father. "If only we had some honey to soothe your throat and make you feel better."

Papa's breathing sounded like a metal spoon grating against a cast-iron pot. His pasty white face made the dark circles around his sunken eyes stand out sharply.

Papa pulled up the woolen blanket to his chin and closed his eyes.

Adam's grandmother, his *bubbe*, arose from her bed and went to look down at her sick son. She shook her head. "You know, my *boychik*," she said, turning to Adam and giving him a tight hug, "from all the troubles in Europe, we escaped to come to Columbus's *goldene medine*—this golden land of America." She paused for a moment to collect her thoughts in English. "Here we enjoy the taste of religious freedom and freedom from those *farshtinkener pogroms*. So terrible were those attacks on Jews! We must count our blessings. But such *tsores* we still have, for we have little money and your Papa is too sick to work."

Adam looked down. The sign "Bieman Tailors—Fine Suits for Reasonable Prices," which had once hung outside the window, now lay inside on the floor beneath the windowsill. Piles of fine wools remained untouched in the corner, and not even half a suit was ready. Wiping a tear from his cheek, Adam turned and filled the central tube of the brass samovar with wood for heating the water. This metal urn was one of the few treasured possessions the family had been able to take with them

when they had left Lithuania so quickly.

Soon the rising steam signaled the hot water was ready, and Adam made the tea for Papa. He noticed that there were only a few sugar cubes left. He handed the china cup and saucer to his father, who was sitting up in bed now, trying to read.

Putting down his book, Papa coughed. "Thank you," he said in a soft, raspy voice, pushing his glasses down his nose and looking up at his son for a moment. Then Papa started to sip the tea.

Bubbe put her arms around Adam and continued her musing. "You know," she said, "from the old country to the new city in America, that was hard enough. Now when we left Orchard Street in New York and moved here to Mountaindale in the Catskills, I thought this fresh country air would help your Papa. But he has only become worse." She looked over at her son and shook her head. "Pray to God that your Papa does not have consumption," she whispered.

Adam shivered. He knew all about

consumption. It invaded a person's lungs. That very disease had in fact killed the mother of one of his friends from the city. He stared at the wooden floor.

Bubbe turned to face him, putting her hands in his. "Your mother and I love to cook for our children. You are our pleasures and our treasures. But we don't have enough food for the winter, not even for *Rosh Hashanah*. The High Holidays will be here soon enough! It is such a terrible shame." She sighed deeply. "Sure Mountaindale is less crowded than the Lower East Side in the city. But who would have thought that today, in 1910 in America, life would be so hard? Even here in peaceful Sullivan County." Shrugging her hunched shoulders, she raised her hands with palms upwards.

"We'll get enough food for the New Year." Adam hugged his grandmother. He had never noticed before how old she looked, with her gaunt face and deep forehead lines.

Then he embraced his mother around her narrow waist as she stood churning butter.

"Don't worry, my *bubeleh*, my dear child," she said.

Adam looked up into her deep eyes, accented by dark eyebrows. Her face was beautiful even with her hair held back in a bun.

"You hurry along to school now," she added as she continued churning with her thin but nimble fingers.

"Somehow, we'll get enough food!" repeated Adam. He shut the door behind him and set off for school.

As Adam walked down the road, he thought about Bubbe's words. He knew that they needed food soon, but what could he do? He scratched his head and tried to flatten his cowlick. *As usual, it is standing straight up like a cornstalk*, he thought. He put on his cap. The brim drooped down to his eyebrows because it was two sizes too big—a hand-me-down from Papa.

Now if Papa does not get better by next week, then I'll have to find work. I'll work for food so that we won't starve. Adam knew that it was not uncommon for twelve-year-olds to help the family by working six days a week, ten hours a day.

He thought of the drudgery it would be. Worse still, he knew that to give up his schooling could ruin his chances of success in America. Moaning, he put his hand into the pocket of his brown knickerbockers and pulled out an old cup-and-ball toy.

Adam quickened his step on his way to school. He tossed the ball into the cup as he ran alongside Sandburg Creek. The water cascaded in white foam over the black boulders of the brook. Adam felt the crisp breeze on his face and heard the birds chirp in the apple trees.

12

Every day Adam passed by the apple orchard on the Friedland farm. The final days of September signaled the time for the apple harvest, and the trees were swollen with fruit. There were so many apples—ripe, red apples—all ready for the picking. Adam's stomach grumbled as he stared. *If I picked one apple, would anybody notice?*

He took one step towards the gray stone wall surrounding the orchard, then stopped, turned, and walked away. Looking around, he put the toy back into his pocket and waited for a moment. The farm was quiet and peaceful. Still, Adam hesitated. Taking a deep breath, he jumped up and grabbed onto the top of the stone wall. His sweaty palms slipped, and he fell back. But the growling in his stomach reminded him of his hunger. Wiping his hands on his pants, he jumped up again. This time he was able to hoist himself up. Once on top of the wall, he straddled his legs to gain his balance.

As he plucked an apple from the tree, the wind blew noisily. Adam huddled under his jacket and wrapped his scarf around his neck. He held the red apple firmly in his hand. His heart pounded. As he was about to slide down the stone wall, the wind suddenly subsided.

Perhaps I could take another apple from the tree, he thought. *Surely no one would see me so early in the morning.*

In the stillness that followed, Adam snatched a second apple from the tree. A blast of cold wind, stronger this time, swept through the orchard, bending the branches low. Adam clutched his cap before jumping down onto the dirt. Sliding both the apples beneath his cap, he bolted from the farm. He turned right at the end of the grove and disappeared into the thicket opposite it.

Pushing his way through the dense undergrowth, Adam came upon a cluster of trees. He sat down in the grass, leaning back against the trunk of an old elm. As he took one apple from beneath his cap, his mouth watered and his stomach growled.

Adam took the first bite of the fruit. It was crunchy with a hint of tartness.

The apple seemed to him the most delicious one that he had ever eaten. Juice ran down his chin. *Only one bite*, he told himself. *I have to save some for Papa.* But he took another bite and then another. Soon he had finished the apple. Wiping his mouth with the back of his hand, he tossed the core into the bushes and tore off to school.

2

A Lesson to Learn

Once Adam climbed over the hill, the white schoolhouse came into view. The one-room wood-frame building served all the children from the small village. Adam opened the door slowly. The young teacher, Miss Elliot, was reading to the class.

"Adam," she said in a stern voice, "I am glad to see that you have decided to join us." Clearing her throat, she asked, "Why are you so late today?"

"I was caught in the thicket," Adam said. "My stomach ached," he added, "so I had to sit down for a few minutes."

As Miss Elliot was a teacher whom he respected, Adam could not look up at her. Instead, he stared at her long green skirt.

"Kindly take your seat and remove your cap."

Adam edged up to the teacher. "My hair is sticking up like a stalk of corn,"

he whispered. "I'm training my hair to stay down."

"Very well then," she replied, with a hint of a smile.

His eyes followed the uneven floorboards until he reached his desk. Adam nodded to his friends Daniel, Jacob, and Abraham.

"What are we reading?" Adam asked Jacob.

"*Poor Richard's Almanack*," came his reply.

Adam sat down and began reading. Soon he was immersed in Benjamin Franklin's book. Miss Elliot explained why this book from the eighteenth century was still important today. Not only did Benjamin Franklin help draft the Declaration of Independence, but he also had great wisdom.

Adam felt his face turn red as he read the words in the text:

> *None but the well-bred man knows how to confess a fault, or acknowledge himself in an error.*

"Want to play baseball after school?" asked Daniel, holding up his book to hide his face.

"Not today. Papa is still sick and I need to go straight home," answered Adam.

"When I am ill, Mama always makes me a *goggel-moggel*," said Daniel.

"What's that?"

"Sounds like a Jewish turkey gobbling!" said Jacob, snickering.

"Now let's talk turkey." Abraham spoke in a slow, low voice. "I mean, let's talk business here."

The four boys held up their books, hands over their mouths, muffling their laughter.

"What the heck is a *goggel-moggel* anyway?" asked Adam again.

Wiping a smirk from his face, Daniel said, "A get-well mixture of some hot milk and an egg. It's good for sore throats."

"Thanks," replied Adam, forcing a smile. "We should try that!"

When the bell rang at the end of the school day, Adam rushed out the door and hurried down the dirt-packed road. When he passed by the Friedland farm for the second time that day, he stopped. The apples in the orchard glittered in the late afternoon sunlight like shiny copper globes. But the dark branches of some of the trees reached out like angry fingers pointing at Adam's misdeeds.

An icy chill ran down Adam's back. He raced home so fast that his feet barely

touched the ground. When his grand-mother opened the door of the small wooden house, he took the apple from beneath his cap and tossed it into her welcoming hand.

"Here, Bubbe," he panted. "This is for Papa."

"Why, my *boychik*, you are so kind to think of your poor Papa," she said. "He is weak and coughs like a neighing donkey with this mystery illness! To eat an apple, it will do him good."

His father peeked out from the mass of blankets wrapped around him. "Adam, such a nice boy you are to think of me. But no, thank you. I don't want anything to eat, not even an apple. It's hard and will get stuck in my throat, which is very sore."

"Papa! Papa! I almost forgot!" Adam said in an excited voice. "Daniel told me about a *goggel-moggel*. It's supposed to be good for sore throats." After a pause, he added, "Can I make you one? We have some milk and an egg."

"No, thank you, my *boychik*," his

father replied.

Adam's heart sank. "I want you to get well, Papa. I hear the winters can be so harsh and cold here! Worse than in the city."

"Yes," said Papa, wiping his brow. "But I am still so tired and weak." He paused and cleared his throat. "I must try to do some work, even for a few hours a day. Otherwise, nobody will have a new suit for the High Holidays."

Adam's mother, standing nearby, ran her fingers along a bolt of black woolen fabric. "I know that you are the best tailor in Mountaindale," said Mama, "but you are ill, and you cannot make good suits right now."

"I must work," he insisted, his voice barely above a whisper. "I don't want to lose all the business for the High Holidays. People have heard of my suits all over Sullivan County, and still, in the city, men want to buy Bieman suits. It is my busiest time of year. Without me, the men here will take the O & W Railroad

to New York. Taking the train to the city and paying high prices for those fancy suits!" Lowering his head, he sighed. "I cannot allow that to happen. I must get better now."

Adam glanced towards the corner where the cloth lay piled high, untouched.

"It doesn't matter, Papa," said Adam. "They can wear their old suits for the New Year. They don't need to take the Old and Weary to the city."

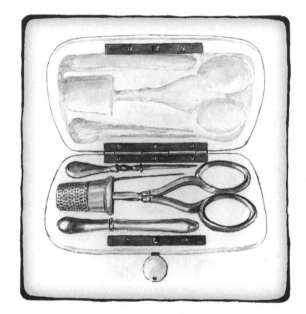

The corners of Papa's mouth broke into a smile. Still, he shook his head.

"You must get well first," insisted Adam. "Then you can make some more suits."

Suddenly Papa looked discouraged. "Mama is right. Only *schlock* suits can I make," he said in disgust. "Only shoddy, poor suits, when I am so sick. These are not my normal superior suits. These are not the Bieman style!"

"*Oy vai iz mir!*" Bubbe wailed to Papa.

"What do you mean?" cried Mama, tucking up the strands of long black hair that had escaped from her bun. "We all

have *tsores* enough. Especially people who do not have enough food."

Adam followed Mama and Bubbe into the kitchen, where Bubbe slumped into her mahogany rocking chair and wrapped her white shawl around her shoulders. "We must find a way," she said.

Adam looked at Mama and Bubbe. They both just sat there, eyes downcast, smiles turned upside down.

"*Nu?*" said Bubbe, breaking the silence. "Well. We must not fail Papa now."

"You're right," cried Mama. "We did not come all the way to America to be defeated by hardship because of Papa's sickness. Bubbe and I can help finish some suits."

His grandmother nodded. "Sure, we can give him some help." She rocked back and forth in the chair.

"Bubbe," said Adam, "can you also help make something special for the New Year if Papa doesn't want the apple?"

"For Rosh Hashanah?" Bubbe thought for a moment. "A special dessert? It is

true. Rosh Hashanah is almost already here," she said and smiled. "Mama and I can make an apple cake. We must use our delicious family recipe."

"We need at least six apples to make the cake," said Mama. "Adam brought home only one."

"I can get five more. For free," Adam blurted out, excited at the mention of the dessert.

"Where do you get such a fruit that doesn't cost you any money?" asked his grandmother, her voice soaked with suspicion.

"I found it on the ground," he lied, scrunching up his toes. "Some apples had fallen over the wall of the orchard."

Smiling, Bubbe clapped her hands. "Apple cake for renewal; apple cake is a jewel!"

"Then it is settled! We shall bake a wonderful apple cake for the New Year,"

said Mama, wiping her hands on her white apron and giving Adam a hug. "And to make the cake taste the best, we can top it with some brown sugar and caramelize it."

Bubbe smacked her lips. "Such a cake we'll make! Mama and I can bake the best apple cake for the New Year."

"What do you put in it?" asked Adam.

"I don't know anything from recipes, my *boychik*," said Bubbe, "but we put in apples, of course, some eggs and some butter, a handful of flour, another handful of flour, a squeeze of lemon, *a bisel* sugar, just a little, then add some almond essence."

"It will be the most delicious dessert ever served for Rosh Hashanah," said Mama, her brown eyes brightening.

Adam smiled at them, but his excitement was already giving way to uneasiness.

3

A Strange Storm

The following morning, Adam went about his chores as silently as a mouse looking for a morsel of cheese in between wooden planks.

"Sweeping is great fun," whispered Adam to his sister, Sarah, as she played with her paper dolls. "Look, you can pretend that you're dancing," he said, swishing the broom and twirling around. "But you must not make any noise to wake Papa."

"No, thank you," she said. "I don't feel like pretending anything. Even my paper dolls are sad because Papa is sick."

Just then, Mama walked into the house carrying a bucket in each hand. "I have some warm milk and fresh water for you children," she said. "But we have to make do with just a little bread for breakfast."

"Fresh milk from the farmer's pail!" Adam gave her a big kiss.

20

Mama put a ladle into the bucket and poured some milk for both of them.

"Dunk the bread into the milk to make it soft," said Adam to Sarah.

She dunked a piece of bread and gobbled it down. "I'm still hungry," Sarah moaned, rubbing her stomach. Her dark, curly hair seemed to droop along with her frowning face.

Mama shrugged and shook her head.

"Here, take mine," said Adam, giving his bread to his sister. "I have to leave early for school today anyway." He patted down his cowlick, but it popped back up. Muttering under his breath about his cornstalk hair, he put on his father's old cap.

Adam shivered as he shut the door behind him. His father's cough was no worse, but still no better. As he walked, he resigned himself to finding work. No more would he play with his friends. No more would he dive into piles of fall leaves or play baseball after school. No more would he sneak off the road to pluck those brilliant red apples from the Friedland farm—at least not until he had picked all six apples for the apple cake. Then Papa could have a piece. The soft cake would be perfect for him to eat.

Thinking about the delicious fruit sent chills down Adam's spine. It was wrong to take those apples. His stomach churned, but his stride became swift. Bracing himself against the morning chill, he hurried down the road. As he approached the apple orchard on the Friedland farm, the trees swayed in the gentle breeze. The sunshine brushed the red apples with a bright glaze. Adam glanced at the ground. Of course, no apples had fallen outside the stone wall of the orchard.

Taking a deep breath, Adam climbed the wall. Then he grabbed a branch and plucked a ripe apple from the tree. A strong wind blew. Straddling the stone wall, he gripped it with both hands and ducked to avoid the gust. As he did so, he dropped the apple. He let out a cry as the fruit fell to the ground with a thud.

The farmhouse was a short distance away. Seeing that no one stirred, Adam became more confident. He plucked two more apples. He then jumped down inside the orchard. Crouching against the stone wall for protection, he waited for the wind to stop. It did not. Then a clap of what sounded like thunder broke through the blue sky. Adam shuddered in disbelief. He scooped up the dropped apple from the ground and popped all

three apples beneath his cap.

The thunder continued to rumble as Adam climbed back over the stone wall. He headed towards the thicket to avoid the storm that seemed to be chasing only him.

Reaching the familiar safety of the thicket, Adam collapsed onto the grass by the trunk of his favorite elm. His heart beat so fast that he thought it might burst. Swallowing hard, Adam noticed the fuzzy texture of his tongue. His mouth was exceptionally dry. Slowly, he slipped his hand beneath his cap and took out one apple. His mouth watered as he tasted the fruit. *Only one bite*, he told himself. *I have to save some for the apple cake*. But he took another bite and then another. Soon he had finished the fruit. As he tossed the core into the bushes, he sighed and continued on to school.

Adam arrived tardy again. He peered through the schoolhouse window. The teacher was writing a complicated arithmetic problem on the blackboard. Adam eased the door ajar. Thankful that

it did not creak, he crept inside and tiptoed to his seat.

"Who can work out the answer?" asked Miss Elliot.

By the time the teacher had turned around, Adam had written the solution on his paper. In his haste, however, he had smudged his work.

He held his inky hand up high, almost jumping out of his seat.

Miss Elliot complimented him on the correct answer. "But remember, 'He that can have patience, can have what he will.' Another wise quote from Benjamin Franklin," she said knowingly.

"How come you're so smart then?" asked Daniel, whispering behind his book.

Feeling a strong queasiness in his stomach, Adam shrugged. "Who knows?"

When recess came, Adam, Daniel, Jacob, and Abraham went out to play the cup-and-ball game. Adam pulled the toy out of his pocket, but in his haste he dropped it. He bent over to pick it up, when an apple fell from beneath his cap. *Kerplunk!* It landed on the hard ground.

Adam's cheeks reddened nearly to the color of the ripe fruit. Ashamed, he grabbed the apple and ran to the top of a pile of leaves, burying his face. The other boys followed and started to throw the leaves at one another. Adam was relieved that they made no comment about the apple. Scooping two handfuls of leaves, Adam flung them up in the air and then at the other boys. The leaves fell like soft rain over their heads. They laughed together, their voices silly and high-pitched. Then the boys returned to their cup-and-ball game.

"Adam is surely going to win. He's always playing this," said Daniel.

"He has the keenest eye for the ball," added Jacob.

But Adam was busy thinking about how he could help his father.

I can't put the ball in the cup even though it's attached to a string, he chastised himself, when he realized that he had come in last.

After school had ended for the day, the boys started home together. When they came to the fork in the road, Adam waved goodbye to his friends. He watched them walk up the path until the three figures turned into silhouettes against the dusky landscape. As they disappeared, he felt a lump in his throat.

For the second time that day, Adam decided to stop by the Friedland farm. He could see the apples on the trees shining in the late afternoon sun like mirrored balls, reflecting sunset shades of red, pink, and gold. Work in the orchard had probably ended for the day. Adam thought that he could perhaps take one more apple from the tree by the wall. He was already halfway to getting the six apples needed for the special Rosh Hashanah cake. What a delicious New Year apple dessert they would have!

Adam clambered up the stone wall and stepped onto a shadowy branch. Just as he was grasping an apple from the tree, he heard a voice.

Chapter Three

"Some turkey is eating my apples," said the man with agitation.

Adam lowered his head and hid behind the leaves. The man moved in his direction, coming closer and closer. Shaking, Adam slid down a branch, but his suspenders became caught on a snapped twig. He was stuck! One hand gripped the branch. His other hand clutched his cap, lest those precious apples should fall.

Step by step, the man approached, his feet crunching the dead leaves.

My pants and I are done for, Adam thought to himself in agony.

The man stopped a few feet from the tree. It was the farmer, Mr. Friedland.

Adam waited. He stayed as still as a scarecrow, but his heart thumped like the hooves of a galloping horse. The farmer listened and waited. Then he turned around and headed back to the house. Adam breathed a deep sigh of relief. He freed his suspenders, slid down the branch, and scaled the outside wall of the orchard. Dust flew everywhere as his feet hit the dirt-packed road. He raced back towards his house.

When he arrived home, Adam took the two apples from beneath his cap and

threw them into the welcoming arms of his grandmother.

"Bubbe," he cried, "now we have three apples for the cake. Only three more! Then there will be enough."

"Thank you, my *boychik*. Please God, we shall have a new start for Rosh Hashanah."

Shuddering, he nodded. *I do so hope that I get three more apples for the cake!*

A Narrow Escape

The next day Adam rose early to fetch some logs for the fireplace and for the wood-burning stove.

Donning his father's old cap, Adam went into the woods nearby. In the crisp air, the morning dew on the undergrowth shone like glass beads. Leaves and acorns crunched beneath his feet. Soon he came upon a large chestnut oak with dried branches, which he chopped into logs. He also cut dried twigs from a hemlock

for kindling. When he had gathered enough wood, he returned home. His mouth watered as he imagined the smell of the apple cake cooking in the oven. Putting the wood by the fireplace, he went to check on Papa. Half asleep, his father opened his eyes and forced a smile.

Adam knelt beside the bed and held his hand. "Papa, I hope you feel better before the holidays. Bubbe and Mama are going to bake a delicious apple cake

for Rosh Hashanah," he said, his voice rising with excitement. "Please don't worry about making any suits for the holidays. I can go and work in a cannery for a fruit farm or as a farm hand. Or maybe even in the General Store on Main Street. Then at least we will not go hungry this winter."

"You are a good son and a *mentsh*, but I'll be better soon. For you to give up your education would be like crushing a gold nugget with a pickaxe," Papa said thoughtfully. "Maybe you'll be a doctor when you grow up. Who knows? In America anything is possible."

Adam gave his father a big smile, waved goodbye to the rest of his family, and went on his way.

Apples glistened in the sunlight as Adam approached the orchard. Curling branches seemed to beckon him. Inhaling deeply, he jumped up and peered over the gray stone wall. He could not see a soul.

Adam climbed the wall and grabbed a branch. As he was about to pick an apple, he looked down and saw Mr. Friedland standing right beneath him. The farmer had been so close to the wall that Adam had not seen him when he looked over the top. Wearing a blue plaid shirt and brown dungarees, Mr. Friedland

tended to the damaged trunk of the apple tree. Adam's heart began to beat as fast as a drum in battle.

He gasped. Then he lost his grip and fell to the ground.

Mr. Friedland turned and glared down at Adam. Adam noted his wild black hair and bushy beard, but it was his fuming red face that scared him the most.

Shuddering, Adam leaped over the wall and fled from the farm. He sprinted past the thicket, his feet pounding the road. He never stopped running until he came to the schoolhouse.

Once up the steps, Adam noticed that the class was already in session. Miss Elliot was again writing an assignment on the blackboard.

This time, Adam beckoned to his friend to open the sash window. As Daniel did so, Adam slid inside before the teacher could turn around.

Hurriedly, he opened his book and listened to the recitation.

"As one of the best readers in the class, Adam, can you please read the word that seems to be causing some trouble for Terence?"

Puffing, Adam had no idea of their place. He did not know either the page number or the paragraph. Raising his

head, Adam glanced at Miss Elliot.

The teacher looked at Adam and repeated the question.

Adam said nothing. He simply stared at her long red dress.

"Well?" she asked.

"No, Miss Elliot, I'm afraid I don't know."

"Can you at least sound out the word?"

Adam nodded. "T-h-e w-o-r-d," he said.

The class broke into muffled laughter.

"No, no, no, my dear boy. That is not what I meant!" Disappointed, Miss Elliot sighed. "The word is *yearning*, which means 'longing.' Emma Lazarus wrote this poem to help raise money for the pedestal of the Statue of Liberty monument in New York Harbor. The children of America helped, too, by contributing nickels, through Joseph Pulitzer's newspaper, the *World*. Her poem 'The New Colossus' became more famous when it was placed on the pedestal." She paused. "Very well then, Jacob, would you continue reading?"

Adam found his place in the book and looked at the final lines of the poem as Jacob read.

Adam marveled at the power of the words to show the meaning of freedom.

Give me your tired, your poor,
Your huddled masses yearning to
*   breathe free,*
The wretched refuse of your
*   teeming shore;*
Send these, the homeless, tempest-
*   tost to me:*
I lift my lamp beside the golden
*   door!*

Adam hung his head. He yearned to breathe free, too. He was so thankful to be in America, this nation of religious freedom, this golden land of opportunity. He so wanted to be a citizen. But was he not off to a bad start by taking apples from the Friedland farm?

Adam could not concentrate. He heard the words, but he did not listen. Looking out the window, he noticed a red bird settling on a tree nearby and began daydreaming. In his imagination, Papa was smiling and busy making suits again. And at Rosh Hashanah, they were all enjoying the delicious apple cake . . .

Adam heard little of the lessons that day. Finally, the ringing of the school bell broke into his daydreams.

"You were awfully quiet today," said Jacob, as they walked together down the road.

"I was thinking about Papa," replied

He needed just three more apples! He was so close! Adam quickly scaled the stone wall. He snatched one of the apples and stuffed it beneath his cap. Straddling the wall, he bent forward and waited for the sudden burst of wind to subside. Then he plucked two more apples.

The wind churned fast and noisily, with the mighty gusts now swirling around him. With his head down, he sat on the stone wall and waited for the wind to stop. Soon a clap of thunder sounded through the skies. Adam fought against his fear. Taking a deep breath, he put both apples in one hand. Then, almost defiantly, he plucked another fruit from the tree. *Three for the cake and one more for me*, he said to himself. Another burst of thunder suddenly broke through the now blackening skies. It roared like a bear protecting her cubs. Terrified by the noise, Adam fell to the ground into a pile of branches. The sharp edges scratched his face.

In the fading light, he could barely see Mr. Friedland rushing towards him.

Trembling, Adam could not otherwise move.

The farmer shook his fist and yelled, "Keep out of my orchard!"

With a burst of adrenaline, Adam

Adam. "I pray that he gets well before Rosh Hashanah. I have to hurry home now." As they came to the fork in the road by the orchard, he waved goodbye to his friends.

When he reached the Friedland farm, Adam stopped. He desperately wanted to have the six apples for Mama and Bubbe so that they could bake the best apple cake for Rosh Hashanah. Then they would indeed have a special New Year!

The late afternoon sunlight reflected once again on the apples, dusting them with specks of gold. In the growing darkness, Adam thought that he could hide among the silhouettes of the branches and no one would notice him.

shot to his feet. Despite the farmer's presence, he stuffed the three remaining apples under his father's old cap. Climbing over the wall, he took flight. But he was now crying. To prevent the salty tears from stinging his scrapes, he shut his eyes for a moment.

Adam raced towards the thicket and his favorite elm. He fell at the foot of the tree. Panting, he pulled out an apple from beneath his cap. Only one bite, he told himself. I have to save some for the apple cake. Today, however, he could eat only one bite.

The fruit tasted like a raw potato. With a sick feeling in his stomach, he tossed the apple into the bushes and hobbled home.

5
Another Close Call

When Adam reached his house, his grandmother again greeted him with welcoming arms. He took off his cap and handed her the final three apples for the cake.

"Thank you, my darling," she said, taking the fruit. "But you look terrible. Are you all right?"

"Oh, Bubbe," he moaned.

"*Oy gvald!* Your face! Such a shame! Scratches I can clean for you. A nice glass of milk you want?" She put her arms around him and asked, "You get into a fight at school or something?"

Adam nodded. "Or something . . .," he muttered. "How's Papa?"

Despite Papa's raspy breathing, he lay asleep. His face was drained of color. Forcing back the tears, Adam went to find his mother. Without words, they held each other in a tight embrace.

"You look tired, my son," said Mama,

32

moving away to stir the pot on the wood-burning stove. "Bubbe and I have made a delicious chicken soup for dinner with lots of potatoes and carrots. Sadly, only a little chicken each." She shrugged. "But in the morning, we'll make the cake for Rosh Hashanah—now that we have the six apples. Thanks to you."

Mama picked up one of the brilliantly red apples, which filled the palm of her hand. Studying the fruit, she added, "These look like Jonathans. They are the best for special holiday desserts. They are sweet but a little tart. The cake will be delicious!"

"I know it will," Adam replied softly.

"You do look tired," said Bubbe, holding his face in her hands. "Come, let me clean your face." She dabbed the scratches on his face with a clean cloth and water.

"Ouch."

"You're fine, my *boychik*. It's not so bad. Now let's eat."

"What about Papa?" he asked.

Mama shook her head. Adam sighed.

Then Mama said the *motzi* blessing for the bread.

Adam took a few mouthfuls. He had to eat something or he would offend Mama and Bubbe.

"You do not eat enough," said Bubbe, studying Adam. "Why, your arms are like sticks."

"But, Bubbe, I do eat. I'm just not hungry at the moment." Adam winced. He took another couple of mouthfuls to satisfy his mother and grandmother. Passing his food to Sarah, he then left the table to check on his father.

"Can I make you some tea?" Adam asked, entering the bedroom.

His father slowly shook his head and put his book on the nightstand. "No, thank you, my *boychik*. Mama is already making me some."

She came to his bedside with a cup and saucer in hand. "I have Papa's drink. You go to sleep, my *bubeleh*," said Mama.

"You need your rest, too."

Adam shrugged. He left to wash his face and hands and to change into his nightshirt.

All of a sudden, Papa began crying like a wounded animal. Adam rushed back to the bedroom.

"The pain in my chest, *ay-ay-ay*," he wailed, his breathing swift and shallow. "The p-p-pain in m-m-my chest," he stammered, struggling for air.

Seeing his father this way made the boy weep. Wiping his tears, Adam watched his mother raise his father's arms. "Mama, Mama!" he cried. "Why is Papa shaking? What should we do? How can we help poor Papa?"

"Hurry. Bring me a glass of water."

When Adam returned, he gave the drink to Papa. Spluttering, Papa pushed it away. The glass flew into the air, with water spilling over like little falls. Adam caught it before it fell to the floor.

"Good catch," Mama said, gently moving Papa's torso forward. "Now bring me a wash basin and a towel." She paused and bit her lip to stop herself from crying. "*Oy-oy-oy*, such an illness. I think this is more serious now."

Adam shuddered at his mother's use of such a woeful expression.

Bubbe came to see what all the commotion was about. Upon seeing her son's contorted face, she put her hand to her mouth. "*Oy gvald*," she moaned. "Quick now, Adam. Put on a jacket. Go and fetch Dr. Maxwell!"

"He lives two houses down," cried Mama. "On the left."

"But how will we pay the doctor?"

"Just go! Please, God, we shall find a way."

Adam threw on his jacket over his nightshirt. He flung open the door and banged it shut just as fast. Then he dashed down the street to the doctor. *Lucky it is so close*, he thought. *Oh, God, I pray that Papa will be all right.*

"Emergency! Emergency!" Adam shouted, as he banged on the door. "My father is in much pain. He can hardly breathe."

The doctor, a tall man with a gaunt face, appeared with his black medical bag already in his hand. Grabbing an overcoat and a hat, he was ready to leave at once. Together, they ran back to the house.

Bubbe answered the door. "Doctor, doctor, my poor son. Such a pain he has now in his chest. He breathes so bad like his lungs are filled with stones. *Oy gvald!*

Please, God, no consumption," she cried, wringing her hands.

"Where is your son?" he asked, his voice without expression.

Bubbe showed the doctor to the bedroom, where Papa now lay quite still.

Dr. Maxwell listened to his breathing.

"If I hold my breath for a moment," explained Papa, "the pain stops. But such a pain I never knew!"

The doctor then placed his stethoscope on Papa's chest and listened. Taking an amber bottle from his black

bag, Dr. Maxwell poured out one spoonful. "You will be well again, but you must stay in bed. No work for awhile."

"Ugh!" cried Sarah, scrunching up her face as she peered into the bedroom. "Why does Papa have to take that awful brown medicine?"

"It is pain relief for the trouble in his chest," replied the doctor, walking with her back to the kitchen. Mama, Bubbe, and Adam followed. The physician rolled up his sleeves. "No consumption here, but he does have pneumonia. I shall stay with him through this crisis." The doctor took another medicine from his bag, poured it into a glass, and stirred the mixture. "This should help ease his cough. Also, with plenty of rest and fluids, I think he should recover nicely."

"*Got tsu danken,*" said Bubbe, putting her arms around the doctor. "He should live to be a hundred and twenty."

"I can make again some tea," Mama said. "Papa likes his tea." Then she added, "Some chicken soup, too."

"That should help. Now I must attend to my patient."

Later, when the doctor returned to the kitchen, Mama had heated some water in the samovar and prepared some tea for her husband.

"The crisis period for today has passed," said the doctor. He rolled down his sleeves and put on his overcoat. "Your husband is resting now. But I shall be back to see him in the morning."

"Thank you, Dr. Maxwell. My husband—he cannot work right now," explained Mama. "Such a fine pair of pants he made before he became sick. Still, it is only half a suit. The jacket I am finishing." Pleading with her hands outstretched, she asked, "Would that be payment enough?"

The doctor bent his head and smiled. "Mrs. Bieman, you could have asked the *landsmanshaft*. People here from our village in the old country would have helped you pay for my services. But the trousers would be more than enough for me to see him through this illness. Your husband has a fine reputation for his Bieman suits."

Tears welling in her eyes, Mama smiled back.

As he was leaving, the doctor noticed the six apples on the kitchen table.

"You know what they say? An apple a day keeps the doctor away."

"Doctor, with all this *mish-mash*, with my son's sickness," said Bubbe, looking up at the man, "and moving out here to the country for his health, we are not so ready for Rosh Hashanah. But Adam, he brought us these apples. Now we can make a special apple cake for the holidays."

"Apple cake," repeated the doctor. "I have not had apple cake since last fall. My wife used some apples from the Friedland farm. She bought them from the market here in Mountaindale. Delicious," he said, smacking his lips.

"Bubbe is a wonderful baker. She taught me well, too," said Mama. "We can save a piece or two of the cake for you."

"Thank you," replied the doctor.

Adam scrunched up his toes and blushed. Feeling weak and nauseated, he excused himself. As he passed by the living room, he stopped to look at his father's sewing machine. Slowly, Adam ran his hands across the top. A thin film

of dust remained on his fingers, for the machine had lain idle so long. *It is hard to believe that this little invention, this small piece of metal, can change my family's life so much*, he thought.

Silence was its sound now. For the humming of the busy machine was replaced by the coughing of a sick man.

Adam returned to the room that he shared with his sister and his grandmother. Exhausted, he flopped onto his bed, almost bumping his head on the iron bedpost. That night, he cried himself to sleep.

6
The Truth at Last

Everyone was excited the next morning. Papa would be well soon, and the High Holidays were just a few days away. Mama and Bubbe had the suits almost ready, and Papa could add the fine details as soon as he was better. But now they were making the apple cake. As Adam got dressed, he could hear Mama and Bubbe cutting up the apples.

Bang! Bang, they chopped.

The sweet smell enticed Adam. He hurried into the kitchen to watch the preparations. Sarah poured the lemon juice over the apples in the bowl so they would not turn brown. Mama beat the eggs with the sugar while Sarah added more lemon juice. Bubbe gradually added the flour. Then Mama added the almond essence. Finally, Bubbe and Mama arranged the sliced apples on top of the cake mixture.

"Aren't you happy that we are making this cake a few days early to celebrate Papa's getting better and not having consumption? With your apples *nokh?*" asked Bubbe, pouring the rest of the mixture into the pan. "Is it not *gut?*"

"Yes, it is good, Bubbe. I'm happy that you are making the cake for Papa, but I'm going to be late for school," Adam said, opening the bread bin and tearing off a piece of the stale loaf.

Then Adam went to check on his father. Papa lay asleep, his breathing now softer and shallower. *Rest is a good thing for him,* he reassured himself. *Maybe it just takes time to get well.*

Blowing a kiss goodbye to his family, Adam stepped outside to dreary skies and mist. Even the birds were silent on this gray day. The chill of the morning wind stung the scratches on his face. He tightened his coat around him. Pressing down his cowlick, he muttered, "As usual, it is standing straight up like a cornstalk." He donned his father's old cap, which fell down to his eyebrows.

Soon Adam again approached the Friedland farm. Hurrying past the orchard, he kept his eyes pinned to the road in front of him. Today he could not even look at another apple. He went straight to the schoolhouse, arriving on time for his lessons.

"Adam Bieman! Good morning," shouted Miss Elliot. "I am glad to see that you had no delays today and that you are not tardy!"

"Yes, Miss Elliot," he replied, feeling his stomach fluttering. *Does she know something?*

The teacher's lessons were always interesting to Adam. Today, however, he felt a lump in his throat when she called him to the recitation bench. He had forgotten to memorize the complete text. He could only remember the part of Benjamin Franklin's *Poor Richard's Almanack* that they had studied in class:

> *None but the well-bred man knows how to confess a fault, or acknowledge himself in an error.*

"This is not your usual standard of work," said Miss Elliot.

Adam slunk back to his seat. *Miss Elliot knows so much. Does she know that I took some apples from the Friedland orchard?*

"Better luck next time," said Jacob, patting him on the back. "Keeping your nose in a book like me does have its advantages!"

"You bet."

After school, Daniel asked him to play some baseball.

"I really should go straight home," said Adam.

Daniel examined his bat, feeling the smooth texture of the ash wood. "Makes you proud that these Spalding bats are made right here in Sullivan County."

"Who makes them then?"

"Albert Spalding. He started his business in 1876. Then . . ."

"All right, Daniel Detail," interrupted Adam. "I can play one inning."

The four friends played, with Adam pitching first.

After each boy had batted, Adam said to the others, "I'm afraid I have to go. Papa is ill. He has something called pneumonia."

Daniel looked concerned. "Is that as bad as consumption?"

"I don't think so, but the doctor said that Papa is over the crisis. Thank goodness! He had a bad breathing problem when we lived in the city. We thought Papa's health would improve out here. Fresh country air, you know." Adam bit his lip to stop himself from crying. "Oh well, I must go now!"

"Be patient," replied Daniel. "Good luck!"

"Thanks."

As he passed the thicket on his way home, Adam quickened his step. When he came to the Friedland farm, he picked up his pace even more. *Do not even look at the apples in the orchard. Do not be tempted.* Up the hill he hurried, listening to himself. He dashed by the little shops and ran on and on until he came to his home.

Adam flung open the door.

As soon as his eyes fell upon the kitchen scene, his heart sank. Sarah sat

sobbing on Mama's lap. Beside her sat Bubbe, wiping her eyes.

"What happened?" Adam asked. "I thought you would both be happy now that we know Papa is getting better." He took a deep breath and smelled burning.

"Please tell me." Adam's palms were sweating.

With furrowed brows, Bubbe looked at him.

"The cake!" the two women cried out in unison. Suddenly understanding what had happened, Adam rushed to comfort his grandmother.

"Mama became distracted, taking care of Papa. Such a sickness he has had! She took more tea, more blankets. I was having a little *shlof*, sleeping in my rocking chair. So what happens?" Bubbe asked, her arms in the air. "Our wonderful apple cake is now burnt to a crisp. Completely ruined. Do you know what this means, my *boychik?* It means bad luck. It means a bad New Year and a bad year in all. Such *tsores!* As if we did not have enough troubles with your poor papa being ill." She took a deep breath. "*Oy gvald,*" moaned Bubbe. "Our hopes for a happy Rosh Hashanah smashed into the ground like *gehakte leber!*"

"Bubbe," Adam answered, "they are not smashed like chopped liver. It was just an accident. Accidents do happen." However, Adam himself was not so sure. He shivered. *Could this be my punishment for taking the apples from the orchard on the Friedland farm?*

"Now we have no dessert for Papa or for the New Year." Tears rolled down Mama's cheeks. Then Mama took a deep breath and said, "But still we must have faith and hope."

"Where did you find the apples?" Papa cried out from the bedroom.

Adam felt a pang in the pit of his stomach. He went to his father's bedside and knelt there, hanging his head. He said nothing.

"Where did you find the apples?" Papa repeated, struggling to sit up.

Despite his weak voice, his father commanded respect.

Taking a deep breath, Adam spoke slowly. His voice trembled, for he knew he was now in trouble. "They did not actually fall from the trees in the apple orchard. I er . . . I um . . ." He swallowed hard before speaking again. "I climbed over the stone wall and took the apples. I didn't think that the Friedlands would mind."

"You stole?" his father asked, his face growing red. "It is forbidden! What have you done to this family? Is it not enough that I am ill and we are short of money? We do not ask our neighbors for food. I am a proud man. We do not even ask the *landsmanshaft* for help." Adam's father raised his head before falling back against the pillow. "Must you make things worse by stealing? I am trying to finish the suits with the help of Bubbe and Mama. Here in America, we make our way in the world through hard work and honesty."

"But Papa," implored Adam. "I took the apples because I was hungry. They tasted so good, and we didn't have any special food to make for Rosh Hashanah. Surely Mr. Friedland would not miss these apples. He has so many."

"What? Are you a *meshugene kop?*" Papa asked. His voice lacked strength, but he lifted his arms a little in defiance.

"No, I am not crazy, just hungry. And I wanted to have a happy New Year."

A tear ran down Adam's cheek. "But Papa, I only took nine apples altogether."

Papa winced with pain but continued. "Maybe you are right. When I am so sick, my thoughts are all *farpatshket,* all messed up. Nine is not too many, but nine is still too much." Clearing his throat, he

added, "There is something you must do for Mr. Friedland. Hunger or no hunger, sickness or no sickness, the Bieman family does not steal! We have our honor to uphold."

Adam felt helpless. He did not know how to make Papa feel better, and now he had disappointed him, too.

Papa lowered his head and stared at the floor. "You have made things worse for us," he said, without looking at Adam. His voice was sad and solemn. "Go and make your apologies to Mr. Friedland. Then you must see if he needs your help. You must make up for your wrongdoings. God always knows."

For a moment, Adam waited for Papa to turn and look at him. His father kept his gaze on the floor. Without saying a word to anyone, Adam left the house, banging the door shut behind him.

7
The Terrible Fall

With a heavy heart, Adam ran down the hill towards the Friedland homestead. He knew he had to apologize to Mr. Friedland and make amends to him. *What should I say to the man? Being sorry is not enough,* he thought. *I must show repentance through deeds. But what can I do?*

Just then a loud crack, a thump, and a scream broke through his concentration. Adam looked up. Although it was not yet night, the skies had once again darkened from gray to black. The trees began to sway from side to side. The branches looked like the pointed fingers of Mr. Friedland and Papa. Then it began to storm.

Adam turned up the lapels of his coat and pulled his father's old cap further down his face. His stomach churned. The apple cake was ruined, and Bubbe and Mama were beside themselves with

sorrow. But worse, he had brought shame on his family. Now this storm.

As he came closer to the orchard, screams of pain filled the air. Starting to run, Adam was turning the corner when he heard another agonized cry.

"Help! Help!"

Now he definitely knew that the cries were coming from the Friedland farm. Without thinking, Adam headed straight in the direction of the wailing voice. His heart pounded as he scaled the familiar gray wall. Wiping the rain from his face, he perched on the wall and peered into the apple orchard.

The wind lashed the trees so hard that it ripped leaves from the branches. Through the heavy mist, Adam could see the silhouette of the farmer lying on the ground. Beside him lay his wife and a fallen ladder. He heard Mr. Friedland moaning and Mrs. Friedland crying.

Adam gripped his hat with one hand. With the other hand, he wiped his eyes. Taking a deep breath, he jumped down into the orchard. His shoes squelched in the mud as he stepped towards the couple. "I heard someone shouting. Are you hurt? Can I do anything to help?"

No one answered.

"Can I do anything to help?" he asked again, this time a little louder.

Mrs. Friedland looked up, wiping her drenched hair away from her face. "My poor husband," she wailed. "We lost so many apples this season. He climbed too high on the ladder to try to harvest more of the fruit. The rain made the ladder slippery, and he fell all the way down."

Adam felt a chill run down his spine. He looked at Mr. Friedland on the ground. The farmer had ripped his trousers, and his leg was bleeding. He lay there in a growing pool of blood.

"Quick, my son!" cried Mrs. Friedland.

"What can I do?"

"Go and get Dr. Maxwell. He lives right here in Mountaindale just past the little shops," she moaned. "Now hurry! Please hurry! If he loses too much blood, who knows what could happen?"

Adam shut his eyes. He knew only too well where Dr. Maxwell lived.

"Be a *mentsh*. Fetch the doctor, please. Hurry!" she implored.

"I'll go straight away. I am so, so sorry," he managed to say.

Mrs. Friedland struggled to get up and open the gate for him.

"I'll be back as soon as I can." Adam tried to sound brave, but his tears mixed

with the rain as he ran up the hill toward the doctor's home.

The downpour became heavier and slowed Adam's steps, but he continued on his way. He stopped only once, bending down to rub his aching calves. When he reached Dr. Maxwell's, he banged on the door so hard that he thought the whole structure might come down.

"Emergency! Emergency!" Adam shouted that all too familiar and fearful phrase. Taking a deep breath, he added, "Mr. Friedland is bleeding to death!"

The doctor appeared in an instant. "I have a medical kit in my saddlebag. My horse, Lightning, is quicker without the carriage, my boy. Come! Jump on behind me, Adam."

The horse carrying Dr. Maxwell and Adam was soon racing through the pounding rain towards the Friedland farm. Adam clung tightly to the doctor's waist as the white horse galloped faster.

The wind howled and the trees shook. Streaks of lightning brightened the night sky like flaming torches, illuminating the way.

Adam felt a painful lump growing in his throat. *This mess is my entire fault*, he thought, trembling.

Soon they arrived at the apple orchard. Dr. Maxwell jumped off the horse and knelt beside Mr. Friedland. "Quick, help me get him to a dry place. I can't examine the gash in his leg here. I need some shelter from this dreadful storm."

"The barn is close by," said Mrs. Friedland, running ahead. "I can put a blanket over a bale of hay for him."

The doctor and Adam lifted the farmer to his feet. Mr. Friedland put one arm around each of them. Through the downpour, they made their way to the barn.

Once inside, Dr. Maxwell and Adam lowered Mr. Friedland onto the blanket. The doctor then lifted and inspected the farmer's leg. He cleaned the injury with a sterile pad and applied pressure to the wound.

"He will need some stitches," replied the doctor, his mouth pursed. "The gash is quite deep. He won't be able to walk for awhile."

Adam's heart pounded. His palms were wet with sweat, despite the rainy chill in the air.

"Who will milk the cows and take the milk to the creamery in Hurleyville? Who will take the eggs to market?" cried

Chapter Seven

Mrs. Friedland. "Now all the apples will rot if they are not harvested."

"It's all my fault," said Adam, after a while. He paused and swallowed hard. "I took some apples, and so you had to climb higher up the ladder to get the fruit."

"Why, you scallywag!" cried Mr. Friedland, waving his fist in the air. "Now I recognize you! I would like to hang you in the tree by your hands and let the birds use your hair for a nest."

"Taking our apples! Why did you do that?" asked his wife.

Reddening, Adam lowered his face. "I was hungry, so very hungry. My father is too ill to work, and we don't have enough food to eat." Tears filled his eyes. "I am so sorry," he cried, suddenly bolting from the barn.

As Adam ran, he heard the piercing words of Mr. Friedland, "How can I forgive you?"

8
Some Serious Advice

Adam fled the orchard like a loose colt. Through the rain and towards the thicket he ran. Mopping his eyes, he stopped. Where should he turn? He was too afraid to go back and face Mr. and Mrs. Friedland. He was fearful of the consequences from Mama and Papa as well. Even Bubbe would have harsh words for him. Where could he go? Where could he run? Where could he hide? *God sees everything,* his Papa had told him. *God sees everything,* he repeated to himself. *That's right! I shall go to Rabbi Solomon! He will know what I should do.*

How reassuring it was to Adam that Rabbi Solomon lived in Mountaindale. He was an immigrant from the old country, and he had also lived near Adam's family in the city. The rabbi was indeed a wise and kind man. His home was always open to the small number of Jewish residents in Mountaindale, even

though he conducted his services in the Shulman farmhouse. Someday soon they would build a synagogue on Main Street.

Adam ran down the hill until he came to a long path leading to the rabbi's white house. He knocked and waited.

The rabbi, dressed in a black suit, answered the door. He was an older man with gray hair and a gray beard. A pair of half-moon spectacles lay on the bridge of his nose. He gestured for Adam to enter.

The young boy trembled as he sat on a wooden chair before the rabbi. Adam fought back the tears. *What will become of me?* He could not stop shaking, so he sat on his hands. He looked down at his shoes, for surely the rabbi would see such fear in his eyes. Did he have the courage

to speak to this great man who carried out God's words and teachings?

At last the young boy looked up at Rabbi Solomon.

"What seems to be the matter?" asked the rabbi in a low, comforting voice.

Adam decided to tell him the truth about taking the apples.

Finally, the rabbi spoke. "In my opinion," he said, stroking his beard, "what you have done is wrong. Taking something that does not belong to you is stealing."

"I know now that I shouldn't have done that. But it was only because we were so very hungry. I didn't think that a few apples would matter to the Friedlands. Papa is ill and . . ."

"I understand why you did what you did," said Rabbi Solomon, a knowing expression upon his face. "Compassion is important. Your father is sick, and you do not have enough food. Still, you must not steal. It is so written in the Ten Commandments." He paused and cleared his throat. "What made you come to see me?" he asked.

"Mr. Friedland fell off the ladder while picking apples in the rain. Mrs. Friedland said he had to climb higher up the tree because they had lost so many

apples. It was the same tree I took the apples from. Then Mr. Friedland fell to the ground and cut his leg so badly," sobbed Adam, burying his face in his hands. "I had to run and get Dr. Maxwell, and Mr. Friedland needed stitches. Now he won't be able to work. Who will milk the cows? Who will pick the apples for the harvest?"

"I see," said the rabbi, cupping his face in his hand.

"I first took an apple one day on my way to school," Adam continued. "I was so hungry and the apple was so tasty. Then I saved six apples for Bubbe and Mama and they made a special cake for Rosh Hashanah. Mama was busy taking care of Papa. Bubbe was napping in her rocking chair. Before they knew it, the apple cake was burnt to a cinder in the oven. It was completely ruined. Now Mr. Friedland has a huge gash in his leg. I don't know what is going to happen to him! All because of me! I am so very sorry for what I did. How can I make things right again?" Adam cried. "I did apologize to Mr. Friedland. But then he shouted, 'How can I forgive you?'"

"You are wise, my child, to recognize that you have done wrong and that you need to make amends," said the

rabbi, patting Adam on the head. "For this week before Rosh Hashanah, we say prayers called *slikhes*. These are the prayers for forgiveness." Clearing his throat, he continued, "Now you must also go back to Mr. Friedland. Find out if you can do anything to help him. And ask for his forgiveness a second time."

"But Rabbi Solomon, I'm scared." Adam paused. "There is something else I should tell you."

"Yes? I'm listening."

"Well," said Adam, taking a deep breath. "I'm scared because every time I picked an apple, a wind blew out of nowhere. When I took two apples, a blustery wind went through the orchard." He swallowed hard before continuing. His heart pounded. "When I picked three apples, a clap of thunder burst through a blue sky. After I took four apples, more thunder exploded. It was really loud. The noise frightened me. I fell onto the ground into a pile of branches and scratched my face."

Stroking his beard, Rabbi Solomon looked at Adam. He did not say a word.

The silence worried Adam. He looked down at his shoes again.

"Some things in life are mysterious and cannot be explained," Rabbi

Solomon said. "You are not a bad child, as you feel guilt and regret for what you have done. But what you did was wrong nevertheless." The rabbi pulled his chair close to Adam. "God is quite disappointed in you, but God has great love for you. God is slow to anger and quick to forgive. It is so written in the Torah, in the teachings of the Day of Atonement service."

Breathing a sigh of relief, Adam bent over in his chair.

"Go now again to Mr. Friedland. Tell him that you are sorry," said the rabbi. "Only this time, you must make up for what you did. Make amends and ask him what you can do for him."

Patting Adam on the back, Rabbi Solomon paused and walked toward the window. Then he looked up toward heaven. He turned to face Adam again. "You must not do to others what you would not have them do to you," he said. "By performing a *mitsve*, a good deed, we can make the world a better

place. It is a religious obligation, and it is something that we must do to make a difference."

"Rabbi Solomon," moaned Adam, "I did not do a good deed by taking the apples. I thought only about my family and myself. I wanted us to have a happy Rosh Hashanah with a delicious apple cake." He bowed his head. "I never thought about the Friedlands. Now I have made two families very sad!"

"The High Holidays are soon approaching," the rabbi explained, "and these are the most important days for a Jewish person. They are called the Ten Days of Repentance, or the Ten Days of Awe. You must think how you can become a better, kinder, and more caring person."

Adam swallowed hard. "How do I do that?" he asked.

"You must go back to Mr. Friedland and ask for his forgiveness again," said the rabbi.

"But what if he won't forgive me?"

"Then you must try a third time. But he must forgive you on your third attempt to apologize. If he does not, then you cannot do any more. However, you must make amends for your wrongs. You can help Mr. and Mrs. Friedland with their farm chores. You must also go to your family to ask for their forgiveness. Only then can you ask God to forgive you and show you mercy."

"Thank you, Rabbi Solomon," said Adam.

"Now, before you leave," said the rabbi, "I want to tell you a story about Yom Kippur, the Day of Atonement. It is the most important day in the Jewish calendar, for we make amends for our wrongdoings. We do not eat or drink anything for a day, and we pray in *shul*. I want to tell you a story from the Aggadah. This literature deals with Jewish legends. Rabbi Tanhuma was a very wise man, who said . . ."

"Just like you," Adam interjected.

Rabbi Solomon smiled.

Then the rabbi began, "In Rome a long time ago, there lived a tailor."

"Just like Papa," interrupted Adam again.

Nodding, the rabbi went on. "On the day before Yom Kippur, the tailor went to the market to buy some fish for the last meal before the fasting started. However, only one fish was left. A servant for the governor was there, and he wanted to buy the fish as well. These two men started bidding for the same fish. In the end, the Jewish tailor bought the fish for twelve denars."

"What is that?" asked Adam.

"Coins of ancient Rome. A lot of money in those times," explained the rabbi. "At mealtime, the governor asked his servant why he did not serve fish. The servant told his lordship that the Jew had purchased the last fish. The governor then asked his servant to summon the Jew. When the governor questioned the man as to how a mere Jewish tailor could afford to buy such a fish, the man replied that he *had* to honor the one day that the Jews have to atone for their sins, no matter what the cost. Because the tailor gave him this explanation, the governor told the man that he was free to leave. Finally, God rewarded the tailor for his observance by placing a beautiful pearl inside the fish. When the tailor sold the pearl, he had enough money to live on for the rest of his life."

Smiling, Adam stood. "Thank you again, Rabbi Solomon. I shall remember your words of wisdom."

"*Nu?*" asked the Rabbi. "Well? Are you going back to the Friedlands?"

"Yes, yes, in the morning," he replied.

The rabbi put his arm around him. "I am glad to hear it, my son."

Yet Adam still had a sunken feeling in the pit of his stomach, because of what he now had to do to make amends.

9
A Change of Course

Early the next day Adam arose as usual. Donning his brown knickerbockers, suspenders, and a cream, long-sleeved shirt, he stood in front of the mirror and tried to flatten his cowlick. *As usual, it is standing straight up like a cornstalk,* he thought. He wanted to look presentable for Mr. Friedland. Then he put on Papa's old cap.

Instead of going straight to school, Adam headed for the Friedland farm.

Shaking from nerves, he pulled out the cup-and-ball from his pocket to distract himself. Passing the orchard, he dared not even look at the fruit trees. Then Adam ran up the pathway to the farmhouse. Panting, he knocked and waited.

When Mr. Friedland opened the door, Adam noticed that he was walking with a cane.

Adam gasped and then cleared his throat. "Mr. Friedland," he said, "I am

sorry for taking your apples. Please, can you forgive me? What can I do to make up for what I did?"

"Let me think about it," he said gruffly. He still seemed angry. "Go on off to school now and come by here on your way home."

Adam lowered his head and trudged down the road to school. It was the worst day that he could ever remember. He hardly spoke to his friends. Even Miss Elliot told him that he looked paler than usual. Everything seemed a blur, and he could not concentrate. He was upset with himself. Although he dreaded going back to see Mr. Friedland, he could not rest until he had done so. He finally asked Miss Elliot for permission to leave school early.

When Adam approached the farm on his way home, he realized that he was trembling again. This was the third and final time that he could ask Mr. Friedland for forgiveness.

Adam froze. *How can I face Mr. Friedland? He seemed so angry with me this morning.*

The distant whistle of an approaching train echoed through the Catskill Mountains.

I can bring him a peace offering, he said

to himself.

And with those thoughts in mind, he took off. He raced to Main Street. Then he ran down the road, past the little shops, until he came to the Mountaindale Train Station. He rushed onto the platform, where many people were waiting.

Adam sensed uneasiness among the crowd.

"The train is late. Maybe there's another crash on Red Hill," said a woman.

"You mean bad-luck hill," answered her companion. "But still, I hope not."

Adam knew that Mountaindale was the main station to the Catskills from the city. A delay could indeed mean terrible news. He remembered his family talking about the train wreck of 1904. It happened when workmen were blasting

through rock to double the tracks on Red Hill, and a huge rock fell onto the rails. The train collided with the boulder and then tumbled down the hill.

"But I just heard the whistle moments ago," said Adam, turning around to face the crowd. "I'm certain of that."

Mumbling, a man paced up and down the platform. His furrowed brow conveyed a deep worry that was contagious. Some women began to cry. Minutes passed, and Adam began to worry, too.

All of a sudden, a whistle sliced through the air and broke the tension. Everyone cheered.

Knowing what to expect, Adam waited with his hands held high.

As the train entered the station, the engineer threw coal to the crowd.

This is a grand act of tsdoke, Adam thought, catching a couple of the pieces—*a great gift of charity*. A few more chunks fell at Adam's feet. He filled his cap with the coal, smudging his face as he did so.

A small boy in scruffy overalls came up to Adam. "You are a mighty fine catcher," he said, smiling. "It would be swell if you could spare a piece or two of your coal. I didn't get any."

Adam smiled back. *It is a good thing to be able to give him this coal. And still there is enough for Mr. Friedland.* "Of course," he replied without hesitation.

When Adam put his cap back on his head, it did not droop to his eyebrows. Wiping his hands on his knickerbockers, he set off to confront Mr. Friedland. *Maybe he won't be so mad with me if I give him this coal.*

Adam hurried back down the dirt road to the Friedland farm and on to the orchard. The fruit on the trees now glowed in the afternoon sunshine, and Adam's stomach growled in response.

Adam soon found the farmer sitting in a chair by the orchard. His bandaged leg and wooden cane reminded Adam of his misdeeds.

He took off his cap and offered the contents of coal to the farmer, who surprised Adam and thanked him.

"You know, my *boychik*, the Baron Maurice de Hirsch set up a fund to help us Jewish farmers in America. He said that immigrants have to work. It is the American way! So I shall set you to work," said Mr. Friedland, rising and hobbling towards Adam. "You can pick the apples. Put them in these wooden buckets. My last big market day before

Rosh Hashanah is only a few days away. I will also need you to help me take the apples to market."

"Have you forgiven me then?" asked Adam, his eyes glistening.

"I do believe I have," said Mr. Friedland. "You see, if I held the anger in my heart, it would make me revengeful and unhappy. It would have made me sick, too. Like eating a bad apple." He hinted a smile. Waving his cane in

the air, he added, "Now run along, my boy! You have work to do!"

Adam let out a cry—a combination of joy and relief. He then worked as fast and hard as he could to pick the ripened crop. Spry and agile, he climbed to the treetops and plucked the plumpest fruit. Soon the wooden buckets were brimming with apples.

"Mr. Friedland, you have taught me that we all make mistakes. Now I can

help you pick the best crop. Thank you for giving me the chance to make things up to you."

"Yes," he replied, "the temptation of my apples was your downfall. Yet, you have mended your ways. You have done grand work. Now it is time for you to go home to your family. And take these apples." He pointed to a wooden barrel filled with brilliant red apples.

"Hurray! Hurray! How wonderful!" said Adam, jumping into the air. "Mama and Bubbe can make apple cakes for Rosh Hashanah. Now we can have a sweet year. Thank you! And I can bring back a cake for you and Mrs. Friedland for the New Year, too."

Mr. Friedland nodded in appreciation.

At that moment, a wild turkey landed on the stone wall. It flapped its wings and flew into the apple tree. Apples fell to the ground. Suddenly, wild turkeys appeared from nowhere and began to gobble up the tasty fruit. Their reddish-brown plumage and long, red necks provided perfect camouflage in the autumn landscape.

"I'm not the only one who likes your apples," said Adam, laughing. "These Jonathan apples from your orchard are the best in Sullivan County."

Mr. Friedland smiled and waved his cane at the birds. "So! These are the turkeys that probably ate most of my apples. They must have eaten two or three bushels!"

"Oh!" exclaimed Adam in surprise. He shooed away the turkeys, glad that he alone was not to blame for taking apples from the tree.

Adam turned and gazed into the distance. The blue tranquillity of the Catskill Mountains and the autumnal foliage of the sloping forests stretched protectively around the village in the valley. The setting sun brushed the leaves on the trees with copper hues, while black-and-white cows dotted the green fields. Colors of purple, auburn, crimson, and gold sparkled across the hills. The reflection of the fall trees in the clear Sandburg Creek glowed like flaming candles, and the glistening waters

glided over the black boulders in sprays of white foam.

Facing the farmer, Adam said, "Mr. Friedland, look at this place! This countryside is like a dreamland. You should invite your family and friends from the city to stay with you on this beautiful farm. You can give them good food and fresh air. You could even take in boarders for the summers."

"Yes, this place is wonderful. Your idea is certainly worth considering," he said. "People are already coming up here from the city."

Turning back to admire the vistas, Adam marveled at how God had created such a paradise. Thinking of God, he looked above the mountains towards heaven. He still had to ask God for forgiveness for his sins.

10
The Sweetest Taste

The Bieman family passed the next day in observance of the Sabbath. They went to the Saturday morning service at the Shulman farmhouse. Rabbi Solomon smiled at Adam knowingly, and Adam was reminded that he had yet to ask God for forgiveness.

Adam wanted to say a special prayer for forgiveness in the familiar safety of the thicket by the trunk of his favorite elm. So, on Sunday morning, after finishing his chores, Adam ran to the thicket. He plowed through the long grass until he came to the elm tree. He leaned against the trunk, thinking. Then he slunk down to the ground. The buzzing of bees overhead sliced through the stillness. Adam lowered his head, and tears streamed down his face. "Oh God," he prayed out loud. "I am so very sorry for what I have done. I did not intend to do harm. I am trying to make amends.

I want to make up for my sins, and I want to be put into the Book of Life. I ate the apples because I was so hungry. Please forgive me!"

At that moment a strong wind tore through the thicket, causing the branches to sway and the leaves to fall to the ground like rain. A loud rumbling overhead made Adam jump to his feet. Then a cracking sound pierced the air. A large honeycomb fell to the ground and rolled towards Adam's feet. He edged over to it and peered inside.

As a swarm of bees flew out of the honeycomb, Adam stepped backwards. He watched the tiny insects disappear into the distance. Lying down, he peered again into the honeycomb. No bees remained, only thick, succulent honey. He put his forefinger inside and scooped up some of the syrupy liquid and put it to his lips. It was so rich and smooth—the best honey he had ever tasted! Looking up, Adam noticed other smaller honeycombs in the thicket. Surely they had not been there before!

Despite the chill in the air, Adam took off his coat and wrapped the big honeycomb inside it.

Then he ran as fast as he could to the rabbi's house. The door was open, and in Adam went.

"What does this mean, Rabbi Solomon? What should I do with the honey?" he asked excitedly. "There are many more wild honeycombs like this in the thicket."

"It means," said Rabbi Solomon, his hands on Adam's shoulders, "that God has forgiven you and has given you a gift of the honey."

"And so it should be," said a voice behind him.

Adam turned. His jaw dropped and his mouth opened wide. There was Mr. Friedland, hobbling on his cane. "How did you know to find me here?" he asked.

"I didn't," replied Mr. Friedland. "I only came to see Rabbi Solomon and ask him how I could help your family. You see, Adam, you showed me that you could be a hard and honest worker by helping me with the farm chores. With

your help, I think we can have a bumper crop of apples this year," he said, smiling. "So I want to help your family."

"There is something I want to tell you about Jewish law," said the rabbi to the farmer. "Leave the corners of your fields for the poor; then families can help themselves to the ripe fruit and vegetables." Turning to Adam, he added, "People who steal a loaf of bread, or apples in this case, are not condemned, because they are recognized as hungry."

"Oh, thank you, Rabbi Solomon," Adam said, shaking his hand.

"Let me tell you something," said Mr. Friedland, putting his arm around the boy's shoulder. "Compassion is also most important during the High Holidays. If I hadn't forgiven you, then who would have helped me harvest the fruit? Now you can come with me to market and help me sell the apples."

"Thank you, Mr. Friedland," said Adam, giving the farmer a hug.

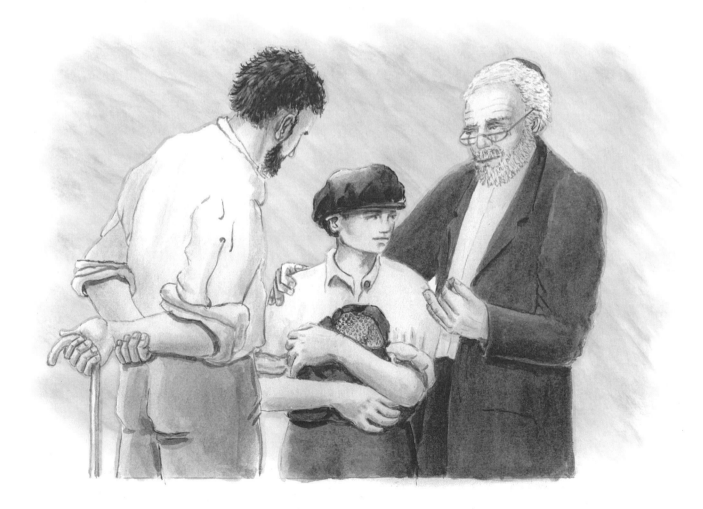

"You are welcome, my son," he replied. "Now it is important that you must also forgive yourself."

Adam nodded. "Does that mean I can keep the honey then?"

"It means that you can keep all the wild honey," said Mr. Friedland. "No one has staked a claim on the land by the thicket."

"Wild honey is known for its healing properties," said Rabbi Solomon. "Taken with tea, it's good for sore throats, and sometimes it can help with respiratory problems, too. I'm not a doctor, but it is an old *bubbe mayse*! It may seem far-fetched, but the drink did help me."

Adam could hardly get the words out fast enough. "Maybe the honey could help Papa get better more quickly. Mama could make him some tea with honey."

The rabbi smiled and nodded.

"Mama and Bubbe can also help me bottle the honey," said Adam. "I can take the jars when I go with Mr. Friedland to market. He'll take the apples, and I'll take the honey."

"The *goldene medine* knows no bounds. Anything and everything is possible! What a business you shall make! Only in America," said Mr. Friedland, with the excitement of a young child. "What a sale we shall have together!"

"All ready for the New Year," said Rabbi Solomon, smiling and stroking his beard.

"Apples and honey," shouted Adam, jumping up and down. "It WILL be a wonderful Rosh Hashanah and a sweet year after all."

Adam rushed home with the honeycomb still wrapped in his coat. When he arrived, Adam placed the honeycomb into the welcoming arms of his grandmother.

"Bubbe," he cried, jumping up and down. "On Friday Mr. Friedland gave me a gift of apples for my honest, hard work. Now God has forgiven me and given me a gift of honey. And we have enough honey to help Papa feel better."

"Thank you, my *boychik*!" she said, giving him a kiss. "Thank God, we shall now have a new start for a sweet Rosh Hashanah."

Feeling a tingle throughout his body, Adam shouted, "Yippee!"

Mama and Bubbe echoed his excitement and hurried off to make Papa some tea with honey. Then they set to work baking apple cakes with the apples from Mr. Friedland. After Bubbe and Mama had finished arranging the layers of apples and the batter, they sprinkled sugar on top. In all, there were enough apples for three cakes. They even had apples left over to make some special apple mousses.

Next, they made three honey cakes. Sarah helped pour the wild honey from the honeycomb into the bowl with the egg and sugar. Finally, they added ground ginger and mixed spices. Now the Biemans, the Friedlands, and the Solomons could all have the delicious desserts for the New Year.

The next night, it was already the third of October and *erev* Rosh Hashanah, eve of the New Year. The chill of the night outside could not lessen the warmth everyone felt as Papa walked

into the kitchen. Adam could hardly believe his eyes. Papa was smiling. His complexion, although not the color of ripe apples, was much improved. Gone was the pain from his face. Bubbe, Mama, and Sarah were smiling, too. Everyone gave Papa a hug before helping him to his seat at the head of the holiday table.

The two round *hallahs*, or egg breads, for Rosh Hashanah symbolized continuity, a circle of life with no beginning and no end. *Lokshen kugel*, a delicious savory noodle pudding; a whole chicken; and some carrot *tzimmes*, or honeyed carrots, completed the feast laid out before them.

"I finished a few suits just in time for the New Year," said Papa in a cheerful voice. "Dr. Maxwell's medicine helped me to get stronger."

"Apples and honey for a sweet year," said Adam, dipping the fruit into the honey. "It's yummy."

"Honey cake, too. But look at the apple cake, much better than before. How delicious it smells!" said Bubbe, her eyes beaming. "Such a cake we did bake with the apples from the Friedland orchard!"

"What a wonderful Rosh Hashanah! I can't wait to eat some," said Adam.

He gave his father a big hug. "But having Papa feel better is the sweetest taste of all!"

THE END

The Catskills Revisited

IN THE BEGINNING CAME THE FARMERS

The Catskills played an important role in American Jewish history of the twentieth century. From 1880 to 1924, about two million Jews arrived in America, the golden land, drawn by both religious freedom and great opportunities. Primarily, these people came from Europe, with the largest percentage from Eastern Europe.

Am Olam, the Eternal People, was one organization that helped new farmers become established. Philanthropist Baron Maurice de Hirsch founded another one, the Baron de Hirsch Fund, which later became the Jewish Agricultural and Industrial Aid Society. Such assistance allowed many immigrant families to settle into farming communities in areas that included the Catskills in Sullivan and Ulster counties. Soon the Catskills had the highest number of Jewish farmers in the nation.

Many of these Catskill Jewish settlers were not used to farming. They were more comfortable with the needle and garment trades, or working as shopkeepers and peddlers. Lacking agricultural skills and the additional funds they needed to operate successfully, some Jewish farmers supplemented their income by converting their farms into boardinghouses. A fair number of residents in the Catskills were not farmers but purchased old farms in order to create boardinghouses. They offered kosher chicken, fresh eggs and milk, rich butter, and home-grown vegetables to their guests from the city.

The majority of Jewish newcomers to America first resided in Manhattan's Lower East Side, living in overcrowded conditions. The small tenements were dark and dank. These conditions contributed to many respiratory ailments. Doctors often recommended that patients, rich and poor alike, move to the Catskills for the health benefits of fresh mountain air.

While the Catskill Mountains appealed to many immigrant groups, this beautiful countryside attracted an entire generation of Jewish vacationers during the twentieth century. Many grand resorts and country clubs developed from such humble beginnings as the Jewish farms in the Catskills.

The High Holidays

There are ten days from the beginning of Rosh Hashanah, the Jewish New Year, to the end of Yom Kippur, the Day of Atonement. These High Holidays are celebrated in the autumn months. Depending upon the Jewish calendar, these High Holidays normally take place sometime between the start of September and the middle of October.

In the days leading up to the High Holidays, Jews get ready in mind, body, and spirit for these Days of Awe. This is a time of introspection. Looking at what they have done in their lives over the past year and how they can make amends for their wrongdoings is part of the renewal process.

Rosh Hashanah celebrates the creation of the world, the beginning of the year, and the start of the penitential season. Apples dipped in honey and honey cakes symbolize the hope for a sweet year. Round *hallahs*, braided egg breads, represent continuity: a circle of life with no beginning and no end. Carrot *tzimmes*, honeyed carrots, are sliced to resemble gold coins in hopes of prosperity. Yom Kippur represents the holiest day of the year, denoted by fasting, repentance, prayer, and charity.

During these ten days Jews reflect upon their good deeds and their wrongdoings. They resolve to right the wrongs of the past. And they pray that God will forgive their shortcomings and inscribe their names in the Book of Life.

Bubbe Bieman's Apple Cake

2 eggs

1 cup sugar

2 cups flour

1 1/2 teaspoons baking powder

5 ounces melted butter or margarine

1 teaspoon almond essence (*optional*)

2 pounds apples

lemon juice

brown sugar for topping

1. Peel and cut up apples. Pour lemon juice over them so that they do not turn brown.

2. Beat all ingredients together into a thick mixture, except apples and brown sugar.

3. Line a loose-bottom cake pan with greaseproof paper around the sides and the base. Put several spoonfuls of the mixture into the pan and sprinkle with the chopped apples. Then alternate layers of the mixture with the chopped apples. Finish off with a layer of sliced apples. Lastly, sprinkle brown sugar on top.

4. Bake at **350** degrees for **1 1/2** hours or until done.

5. Wait for cake to cool before removing from the pan. Place on a wire rack.

Enjoy!

Bubbe Kagen's Honey Cake

1. Beat together the following ingredients:

   1 egg
   1/2 cup oil
   1 cup sugar (1/2 cup brown and 1/2 cup white)
   a pinch of salt
   1 cup honey
   juice from one medium orange

2. Dissolve 1 teaspoon of baking soda in 1 cup boiling water. Let cool until lukewarm. Add to mixture and set aside.

3. Mix the following dry ingredients:

   2 1/2 cups sifted flour
   1 teaspoon ground ginger
   1 teaspoon mixed spice
   1 teaspoon baking powder

4. Make a well in dry ingredients, and pour wet ingredients into dry ingredients. Stir together.

5. Pour mixture into greased pan. Bake for **1** hour at **350** degrees. When cool, cut into squares and store in a cake container.

A sweet start to the New Year!

Grandma Evie's Apple Mousse

1. Peel **6 to 8 apples** and cut into quarters.

2. Put into pot. Pour **one cup of orange juice** over apples.

3. Add **1 tablespoon of sugar** or more, and bring mixture to a boil.

4. Let stew until soft but not mushy.

5. Place in oven dish, and add about **1 tablespoon smooth apricot jam.**

6. Beat **whites of 2 eggs** with **3 tablespoons sugar** until very stiff. Place on top of apples.

7. Bake for **10** minutes in a slow oven (270 degrees). Then lower heat to **250** degrees, and bake for a further **20** to **25** minutes.

Simply delicious!

GLOSSARY

Most pronunciations and spellings are Yiddish words, although some words are a blend of Yiddish and English.

A bisel (ah BEES-uhl) a little, not much

Boychik (BOY-chik) a term of endearment for a boy

Bubbe (BAW-beh) grandmother

Bubbe mayse (BAW-beh MY-seh) a far-fetched tale, an old wives' tale, nonsense

Bubeleh (BAW-beh-leh) an affectionate term meaning darling or dear child

Erev (EH-rehv) the eve before; on the eve of

Farpatshket (far-POTCH-ket) messed up, sloppy

Farshtinkener (far-SHTINK-en-er) stinking

Gehakte leber (geh-HAHK-teh LEH-behr) chopped liver

Goldene medine (GAWLD-en-eh muh-DEE-neh) literally, golden country; refers to the legend among European villagers that America was the land where streets were paved with gold; also, the United States as the land of freedom, justice and opportunity

Got tsu danken (GAWT tsoo DAHNK-en) thank God

Landsmanshaft (LAHNDS-mahn-shahft) organization of people from the same hometown in Europe that provided support for their members with regard to credit loans, burial services, and social and religious services; **landsman** (LAHNDS-mahn) countryman

Lokshen kugel (LAWKSH-uhn KOOG-uhl) noodle pudding

Mentsh (MENCH) a person, usually meaning a good or humane person

Meshugene kop (meh-SHOO-gen-eh KAWP) a crazy person

Mitsve (MITS-veh) a Jewish legal commandment; a charitable deed

Motzi (MOH-tsee) the blessing over bread, recited before a meal

Nokh (NAWKH) yet, still

Nu (NOO) so, well

Oy gvald (oy guh-VAHLT) oh, dear! oh, help! or a cry of surprise

Oy vey iz mir (oy VAY iz MEER) woe is me; an expression of woe

Shlof (SHLAWF) sleep (noun); **shlofn** (SHLAWF-uhn) to sleep (verb)

Shul (SHOOL) synagogue, school

Slikhes (SLIK-hehs) prayers of forgiveness

Tsdoke (tseh-DAW-keh) the obligation to establish justice by being righteous and helping one's fellow human beings. The highest form of charity is to help people help themselves.

Tsores (TSAW-rehs) misery, troubles